The Emperor's New Clothes

A Fairy Tale by Hans Christian Andersen
Illustrated by Christophe Durual

· Abbeville Kids ·

A Division of Abbeville Publishing Group

New York · London · Paris

Once upon a time, there was an emperor who loved clothes so much that he spent all his money on them. He owned so many garments that he changed his outfit every hour! People would always find him in his dressing room.

One day two men came to the city where the emperor lived. They pretended to be weavers who could make the most wonderful fabric in the world. But they were really only swindlers who planned to trick the emperor.

The swindlers claimed that the colors and patterns in their fabric would be more beautiful than anything anyone had ever seen. Even more amazing, clothes made from this fabric would be invisible to anyone who was foolish or unfit for his job.

"Such clothes would be wonderful indeed," thought the emperor. "With them I would know who should and who should not be working for me."

The emperor gave the swindlers a large sum of money to start the job. The two men set up their loom and pretended to weave—without any thread at all.

Soon afterward the swindlers asked for the finest silk and gold threads to finish their work, but they kept the expensive gold and silk for themselves.

Everyone in the city heard about the fabric. People could hardly wait to find out which of their neighbors might be foolish or unfit for their jobs.

One day the emperor decided to find out how the famous fabric was coming along. "I will send my trusted old chief counselor," he said to himself. "He is sure to be able to see the fabric for what it is, since he is so clever and so good at his job."

So the faithful old chief counselor went to the swindlers' workshop, where they were weaving at their threadless loom.

The chief counselor stared at the loom. "This cannot be," he thought to himself. "I don't see anything at all." But he didn't say a word out loud, for fear of looking foolish.

The swindlers invited the chief counselor to take a closer look. They pointed to the empty loom and asked him what he thought of the beautiful colors and patterns. The poor old chief counselor opened his eyes very wide, but he saw nothing at all, for there was nothing to see.

"Goodness gracious!" thought the chief counselor. "Am I a fool? Am I unfit to be chief counselor? No one must know about this."

"Is something wrong?" asked one of the swindlers. "You haven't said anything about our fabric."

"It is charming, utterly charming," said the chief counselor as he adjusted his glasses. "Just look at those patterns and colors! I will tell the emperor that I am very pleased with your work."

And that is what he did.

Then the swindlers asked for more silk and gold threads, which they said they needed for the fabric. But again they kept it all for themselves. They were getting very rich!

Everyone in the city was talking about the marvelous fabric. At last the emperor wanted to see it for himself. He took his most important advisors with him, including the old chief counselor.

"Isn't it wonderful?" cried the chief counselor when they all stood before the loom. "Just look at those patterns! And the colors!"

"What?" thought the emperor to himself. "I don't see anything at all. Am I a fool? Am I unfit to be emperor? Nothing could be worse!"

And so he exclaimed out loud, "Now this is what I call beautiful!"

No one else saw anything either, but they didn't want to admit it. So all of the emperor's advisors agreed out loud that the fabric was beautiful and that the emperor would look splendid dressed in clothes made from this material. He could wear them in the next royal procession.

On the night before the procession, the swindlers didn't sleep at all. By the light of sixteen
candles, the emperor's advisors watched as the
swindlers pretended to remove the fabric from the
loom, cut it with large scissors, and
sew together the pieces. At last they announced,
"The emperor's new clothes are ready."

When the emperor arrived, one of the swindlers
held out his arm, as if there was something on it.
"These are the trousers. This is the coat. And here
is the train. They are as light as a spider's web."

The emperor took of all his clothes and the swindlers pretended to dress him in each piece of the new outfit. Finally, one of them seemed to be attaching something to the emperor's waist. It was the train.

The emperor turned round and round in front of the mirror.

"What well-made clothes!" everyone exclaimed.

"I am ready," the emperor said at last. "I look very grand, if I do say so myself."

Two servants bent over and pretended to pick up the train. They raised their hands and followed the emperor, holding nothing but air.

The emperor led the procession down the main street of the city. As he passed by, people lining the street and watching from their windows cried out, "There is nothing like the emperor's new clothes! Just look at the colors! And what a splendid train he has—it falls so beautifully."

"But he has nothing on!" cried a young child.

"Did you hear what my child said?" the mother proudly asked someone standing near her.

Soon people began whispering the child's words to one another. "He has nothing on. A little child said it—the emperor has nothing on." Finally, everyone was shouting, "The emperor has nothing on!"

The emperor shivered, for it seemed they were right. But what could he do? After all, he was the emperor and people expected him to be dignified. "I must continue to the end of the procession," he thought.

So the emperor stood up just as tall and his servants went on carrying the train that wasn't there.

Look carefully at these pictures from the story.
They're all mixed up.

Can you put them back in the right order?